WELL, I WAS MURDERED IN A LAKE AGAIN

A Novelette By

JASON STEELE

For those we have lost, in lakes, to murder.

"Who could be so lucky? Who comes to a lake for water and sees the reflection of moon."
~ JALALUDDIN RUMI

CHAPTER ONE

The Cold Repeat

The bottom of Blackmore Lake was thick with a grimy, muddy, lifeless silt. Swirls of foul residue slowly circled the lakebed, dimly illuminated by the light of a full moon above. The lake had once been host to a number of fish, amphibians, and other creatures, but in recent years an unknown grayness had taken hold of the water and sucked away its vital essence. Now the lake was host only to death and rot.

Tonight there was a new death for the lake to absorb, a fresh death. Resting in the center of the cold muck, slowly being swallowed up by the silt, was the body of Cyrena Shade. She was a short, stout woman who looked to be in her late twenties, with unruly tangled black hair that was peppered with lines of white.

There was a small hole in her long black dress directly over her heart, out of which oozed a thick, dark, inky blood.

The blood flowed downward into the lakebed as if it were very heavy, disappearing amongst the sludge.

As the bleeding slowed and the last of the color drained from Cyrena, an immense cloud passed in front of the moon above, shrouding the lake in absolute darkness. It was in this darkness that a figure who had been watching the water made their leave, disappearing quietly into the surrounding woods.

An hour passed, and the moon began to reveal itself from behind the cloud. Faint light shone down upon the lake again, the surface of which was gently rippling near the western bank. Lying upon that bank, struggling to breathe and covered from her head to her boots in lake filth, was Cyrena.

She had lain there nearly motionless for half an hour, slowly regaining control of her body. Anyone who saw her might mistake her for a corpse—the color was still completely gone from her skin—but she was alive, and gradually recovering.

There was a delicate pattering of steps in the woods near the lake, and a small gray fox emerged from the shadows. The fox walked along the muddy grass to the edge of the water, and sat themselves about a yard away from the struggling Cyrena. A few moments passed, and then the fox spoke.

"You were dead. Dead and swallowed by a lake which has claimed so many. How is it you continue, human?" The fox's voice was thin and graceful, with an aged but steady tone.

Cyrena opened her mouth to speak, but did not yet possess the strength. The fox sat patiently, awaiting her answer. After some substantial concentration, Cyrena found herself able to utter a few soft words. "This... this is..." she began, her voice hoarse and pained.

The fox listened, unmoving, eyes watching Cyrena with cautioned curiosity.

"This is the second time," Cyrena continued, "that I've been murdered in a lake."

The fox lifted their head slightly, eyes still fixed on Cyrena. "You've died before?"

"Not just died." Cyrena gave a dark laugh, and then choked. "Been murdered. Twice. In a lake." She laughed again, then erupted in a terrible coughing fit.

The fox walked closer, and sat directly next to Cyrena. "What power do you possess, which allows you to return from death?" the fox asked.

"In my entire life I've only been murdered twice. And *both* times were in a *lake.* That's *absurd,* right?" Cyrena pushed her arms into the ground and lifted herself up slightly, looking over at the fox for the first time. "Oh, you're a fox. Okay. Hello." She fell back to the ground.

The fox examined her, watching her body for clues about her essence, about how she was still alive.

"So, uh, do you have a name, fox? You are a fox, right?" asked Cyrena.

"I am a fox. You may call me whatever you wish."

"Alright. Gwendoline."

"Do not call me that. I do not like that name." The fox's voice became slightly testy, and less ethereal.

"How about Heathcliffe?"

"No."

"Anastasia?"

The fox shifted uncomfortably. "I think maybe I do not like human names. Just call me Fox."

"Some humans go by the name Fox, you know."

"Why would you tell that to me? Now I don't want to be called anything. I am nameless."

Cyrena tried to sit up, but her chest was still hurting too much. She turned her head toward the fox and asked, "What about Nameless?"

The fox looked at the ground, and seemed to be contemplating this suggestion with great sincerity. "Yes," said the fox. "You may call me Nameless. It is a paradox. Yes."

"Great. Did you happen to see who murdered me, Nameless?"

Nameless looked at Cyrena, and then over at the woods. "Yes, although I could only see their silhouette. They were small, and still. A hunter, it seemed. They waited, watching you, and then fired a single shot from their rifle into your heart."

"Ah. Creepy. Thank you, Nameless." Cyrena tried again to sit up, but instead fell over on her side.

"Will you tell me how you survived death?" asked Nameless.

"I didn't realize there were foxes who could talk. What kind of fox are you, Nameless?"

"If you do not wish to reveal your secrets, that is your choice. It was interesting to meet you, and I wish you well." Nameless stood up, and began walking toward the woods.

"Nameless. If you help me find my killer, I'll tell you why the killing didn't stick."

Nameless looked to the right, at a clearing in the forest.

"Follow that clearing, and you will find a cabin. A woman lives there. She is kind to the animals of these woods, and I believe you will be safe there while you recover. I will visit you again."

With that, Nameless sprinted off, disappearing into the trees and shadows.

CHAPTER TWO

Cabin of the Doctor

Dawn broke over the forest, and the early twilight illuminated the treetops with a rich, orange light. There was a wide path cut through the trees, and at the end of the path stood a sizable old cabin built out of large gray stones, tinged slightly green by a thin layer of moss. Behind the cabin sat a messy pile of firewood under a tarp, and a small vegetable garden that seemed poorly plotted but otherwise well maintained. In front of the cabin, no longer hidden by the night, was Cyrena, who had managed to make it all the way to the porch steps before passing out.

The cabin was owned by Dr. Piper Calarook, a remarkably tall woman with long, thin, almost spider-like limbs. She had thick-rimmed, cat-eye shaped glasses, and kept her auburn hair pulled tightly back in a short ponytail. She had a very professional look about her, especially for someone who lived in a cabin deep within untamed woods.

When Piper opened her front door in the morning

and saw Cyrena sprawled on the ground, grimy and unconscious, she let out a horrified gasp and assumed her to be dead. A quick check of her pulse told Piper that was not the case, and after unsuccessfully trying to wake her, she carefully lifted Cyrena off the ground and brought her into the cabin.

It wasn't until late in the afternoon that Cyrena finally awoke. Groggy and confused, she slowly sat up and tried to make sense of her surroundings. She was on a padded cot, in the middle of a living room between two mismatched sofas. There were notebooks and papers stacked messily on both sofas, and a few cups of half-finished water resting on an end table to her right.

Cyrena's black dress was gone, as were her black boots, replaced with a burgundy bath robe that was decidedly too long for her. She had been sponged down, too, and was no longer quite as covered with lake silt.

"You're awake! Hello!"

Cyrena twisted toward the source of the voice and saw Piper, sitting on a large oak stool at a writing desk. Piper bolted off the stool and walked over to the padded cot.

"Heeeeyyy there," said Cyrena, wincing slightly at a pain near her heart.

Piper knelt down in front of Cyrena and shined a small flashlight into her eyes. Even kneeling, Piper towered over her. "My name's Piper, I found you outside the cabin. I thought for sure you were dead! How are you feeling?"

"Not great. Pretty sad. Don't really want to talk about that, though. My name's Cyrena, by the way."

Cyrena held out her right hand for a handshake. It

took Piper a second to understand what was happening, but once she did she awkwardly reciprocated.

"Thank you for, uh, whatever you did for me," said Cyrena.

"Oh! Yes, of course. I'm a doctor. Veterinarian, specifically. I really thought I was going to have to operate on you, because of that big hole in your chest and back. But it all sort of healed up on its own, so..."

"Yeah," said Cyrena, rubbing the spot on her chest where a wound had been. There wasn't even a scar there now, although the area still felt sore. "It seems to be all hunky-dory."

Piper paused for a moment, looking nervous. "I'm sorry, I don't mean to be rude, so I'm very sorry if this is rude, but..." Piper leaned in slightly, and her voice got very quiet. "Are you..." She leaned in even closer, her voice lowering to a whisper. "Are you a vampire?"

It was at that moment Cyrena noticed all of the curtains in the cabin had been closed tightly shut, and the one window that didn't have a curtain had been hastily covered with paper and tape. "I should go. Yeah. I should leave. Thanks for everything..." Cyrena tried to get up from the cot, but immediately felt an oppressive dizziness and fell right back into it.

"Oh no! I'm sorry! You don't have to talk about your... situation, or whatever. I won't bring it up again. Please, stay here until you're feeling better. I'm sorry. Gaaahhh..." Piper smacked her hand into her face and stood up, looking around the room. "Can I get you something to eat? Or drink?"

"I could eat."

"Great! I have a stew. It's a little bland, but *extremely* nutrient rich."

"Okay. Sounds good. And nutritious."

Piper ran to the other side of the room, where there was a small kitchen. She took a pot out of the refrigerator, placed it on the stovetop, and began to heat it. Soon the cabin smelled heavily of cooked vegetables.

"I grow my own vegetables out back," began Piper. "I was never any good at growing things, but apparently I've gotten much better living out here." She paused. "Oh, this stew, it uh, doesn't have any garlic in it. Just so you know."

"I'm not a vampire," said Cyrena, agitated.

"Oh! Okay! But just so you know, if you were a vampire or something similar I'd be totally cool with it."

"Great."

Neither of them talked again as the stew heated up, and they continued not talking while they ate. The stew was indeed quite bland, but Cyrena was extremely hungry and it felt good to be eating. Two bowls of stew later and she felt strong enough to stand up again.

"Well," said Cyrena, "thank you for the stew. And for all the help. But I should probably mosey on out of here."

"I'll get your dress! I was going to clean it and patch it, but it… well, the dress did all that by itself." Piper started to walk across the room to get the dress, but then abruptly stopped, her hands fidgeting nervously. "Did you come here for the lake?"

Cyrena stared at her, inquisitively. "Yes. I did."

"Are you here to… do something about it?" Piper realized how fidgety she was being and tried to hold her hands in a natural, still position by her side, but this made her look even more nervous.

"I'm not sure what I'm here for yet. What do you know about the lake?"

"It used to be a regular lake, but at some point it went… *wrong*. Just standing near it creeps me out. Like it's watching me. Like the lake is watching me. The lake couldn't be watching me, could it?"

Cyrena thought about how to answer. "The lake isn't watching you. It's a lake. But it's a very, very bad lake, and you should probably stay away from it."

"I can't!" said Piper, loudly, and then she made an effort to lower her voice to a calmer tone. "Too many animals end up hurt over there, and they're good animals. I'm very protective of them."

"You shouldn't stop doing your vet thing, but I don't think you understand exactly how super bad that lake is."

"Were you going back there? To the lake? We could go together! I know the place pretty well, maybe better than anyone. I can show you where my dog is buried! She loved the lake, when it wasn't horrid. I'm sorry, I'm rambling. You probably want to go alone, anyway."

Cyrena really did want to go alone, but a set of experienced eyes could be helpful. The lake was bad, Cyrena knew that, but she didn't yet know what made it bad, or the full extent of its badness. Also, there was something about Piper that seemed deeply sad, and Cyrena connected very strongly to that. Happy people had always creeped her out, but gloom she understood. "You know what? Sure. Yeah. Let's go to the lake."

CHAPTER THREE

Clues at Blackmore Lake

The forest was eerily quiet—there was no breeze that day, nor were there any calls from birds or insects. The only sounds to be heard were the sloshy footsteps of Cyrena and Piper as they walked down the increasingly muddy path. Piper was wearing brown hiking boots, khakis, and a dark blue half-zip top, and Cyrena had put on her black boots and her mysterious black dress, which had indeed miraculously restored itself.

"Your dress," said Piper, "is very black."

Cyrena's dress was indeed very black—it was the blackest thing Piper had ever seen. It was so black that it had no discernible texture, and was almost upsetting to look at. It seemed to absorb all of the light that hit it, making it look less like a dress and more like a dress-shaped hole in the universe.

"Yeah, it's *pretty* black," said Cyrena, unhelpfully.

Piper had lots of questions about the dress, but she knew that Cyrena didn't want to talk about it.

"Be careful," said Cyrena as the lake came into view. "Besides the lake itself being dangerous, I was here last night and someone shot me."

"*That's* what the hole was? Oh my god, how awful. Do you think they…" Piper stopped herself from continuing.

"Do I think they *what?*" asked Cyrena.

"Do you think they knew? That you're magic? Is that why they shot you?"

"I don't know who they are, or why they did it. And I'm not magic. If anything, I'm cursed."

They had reached the lake. The water was still and dark, and there was an unpleasant sulfury smell in the air. Floating atop the opposite end of the water was an old derelict row boat, which was heavily stained with both lake residue and blood.

"I was on that boat in the middle of the lake when I got shot. I don't remember which way I was facing."

Piper looked at the surrounding trees, her eyes furrowed in thought. "You had a hole on both sides of you, so whatever you were shot with passed all the way through your body, and might have ended up lodged in one of the trees. If it did, maybe we can find the bullet!"

"That's smart thinking, Piper."

"I read a lot, about detectives. Detectives who were murdered on the job. It's a hobby. That sounds like a weird hobby. I'm sorry that I started talking, and am still talking."

Cyrena and Piper split up and began checking the trees for bullet holes, but the trunks of the trees were very shabby and irregular, so finding a bullet in one of them was seeming more and more like a hopeless task. Not to mention that there were hundreds of trees to check, and for all they knew the bullet could've simply ended up stuck in the ground somewhere.

As Cyrena checked her twentieth or so tree, she noticed a small brown squirrel standing nearby, watching her curiously. When she walked to the next tree the squirrel followed, and then continued following her every time she moved to a different spot.

"Hello, squirrel," said Cyrena, in the most casual voice she could muster while talking to a squirrel. The squirrel's ears twitched for a moment, but there was no response. Cyrena knelt, and was now barely a foot away from the animal. "We're looking for a bullet. We think it might be lodged in one of the trees. Can you help us?"

The squirrel dashed forward, and climbed onto Cyrena's bent leg. "Yes, I know where the bullet is," said the squirrel in a low, hollow voice.

"Oh. Great. Can you show me?"

"Yes, I will show you the bullet. But first, you must listen to my greatest, most terrible secret." The squirrel's eyes stared intensely at Cyrena.

"Okay, sure. What's your terrible secret?"

"I once invited my brother to feast upon a bounty of pecans that I had stolen from the kind doctor's cabin." The squirrel looked over at Piper, who was checking trees near the other end of the lake.

"I won't tell her about your thievery. It's a hard life for a squirrel, I'm sure."

The squirrel looked back at Cyrena. "When my brother

arrived for the feast, I smashed his head with a rock, and slowly ate away the meat from his face."

This was not the terrible secret that Cyrena was expecting to hear, but she tried to keep the surprise out of her voice. "You ate your brother's face?"

"I ate all of my brother's face, and his whole meaty head, slowly, as he died." The squirrel's tiny paws began to twitch excitedly.

"That is indeed a terrible secret," said Cyrena. She wasn't sure what sort of reaction she was expected to give.

"That is not the entire secret," said the squirrel.

"Oh. Go on."

"I felt guilt for killing my brother, yes, a tremendous and burrowing guilt. But I also felt a tremendous yearning for more face meat. Nuts and berries could no longer satisfy me, even though they were once all that I craved. And so, I began to attack other squirrels during the night as they slept, consuming their faces and hiding their disfigured bodies in the lake."

"Mmhmm." Cyrena still wasn't sure how she was supposed to react to any of this.

The squirrel inched forward on Cyrena's leg. "Soon, squirrel faces were no longer enough to appease my dark appetite. I buried what remained of my guilt, and moved on to other, more delectable creatures. Chipmunks, birds, frogs…"

"Does this story end with you lunging at my face and trying to eat it?"

The squirrel stood silent, unmoving. "No."

"You're lying. That's totally how your story ends."

"Well not *anymore,*" said the squirrel, indignantly. "Not when you already know the punchline."

"Well that was a very spooky secret, squirrel."

"Whatever. Follow me," said the squirrel, sounding frustrated and disappointed.

The squirrel leapt off Cyrena's leg and began running across the edge of the forest, eventually stopping in front of a particularly knotty looking tree. They scuttled about halfway up the trunk, and began digging into a small hole in the bark and wood. Cyrena watched tensely as the squirrel pulled out a tiny, round, metallic object.

"I don't really eat faces, I was just trying to frighten you, human," said the squirrel, handing the object over to Cyrena.

"I know," said Cyrena, examining the shiny metal projectile with her fingers.

"Well, good luck with your life," said the squirrel, who hurried down the tree and darted deep into the woods.

Cyrena waved to Piper, who was now on the other side of the lake. "I found it," she yelled, and they both began walking toward each other, circling the water's edge.

The forest was still dead silent, and the lack of wind gave everything an uncomfortable sense of dormancy. Being here didn't feel real, Cyrena thought. It felt like being stuck in a dreary painting.

"I can't believe you actually found it!" said Piper as they reached one another. Cyrena held out the metal object, and Piper grabbed it excitedly. After examining it for a moment, she put her hand over her mouth in shock.

"What? Do you recognize it?" asked Cyrena.

"No, it's just... I'm not 100% certain but..." Piper sounded very worried.

"What is it? Tell me, Piper."

"I think this is silver."

Cyrena snatched the bullet out of Piper's hand. "What? Silver?"

"I can test it back at the cabin, but I'm pretty sure that's silver. Someone shot you with a silver bullet."

Cyrena's face twisted in annoyance, and she looked angrily at Piper. "I'm not a werewolf, either." Her expression changed, however, as a memory flickered into focus inside her mind—a memory from her first death. A memory of the large wolf who had tried to escort her into the afterlife.

CHAPTER FOUR

The Healer's Mangled Heart

The sun was beginning to set as Cyrena and Piper returned to the cabin. The moment they arrived Piper ran to her desk and took out took a small, clear bottle filled with an amber liquid. She twisted off the cap, and carefully dripped some of the liquid onto the round metal bullet. It fizzed for a moment, and then began to change color. "The acid is turning red," she said to Cyrena. "It's definitely silver. A very pure silver, too."

Cyrena sat on one of the sofas in the living room, contemplating the meaning of the silver bullet, while Piper heated up a three-bean chili from the fridge.

"This does have garlic in it," said Piper. "A lot. Too much, maybe. So I hope you like garlic!"

It was too much garlic, but Cyrena was too preoccupied with thoughts about the bullet to care. Why was someone in the woods hunting with silver bullets? And why had they shot *her?* Was there someone out there who knew what she was? If so, why didn't they know that silver wouldn't make a difference?

"The lake used to be really pretty," said Piper, as she ate her chili. "That was a long time ago, though."

"How long have you lived here?" asked Cyrena, rolling the silver bullet between her fingers.

"This was my parent's cabin, we used to come here during the summer when I was a kid. The lake was just a lake then. I started coming back here as an adult after they died."

Cyrena stopped rolling the bullet. "Sorry about your parents. That sucks."

"Yeah. This cabin became a nice getaway spot for me and my partner, Tyler. Then a few years ago she got cancer, and now she's gone, too. Even my dog died! Everyone... died."

"Man. I'm... I really don't know what to say. I'm sorry, Piper."

Piper sat herself closer to Cyrena. "Can I tell you something totally irrational? Totally absurd?"

"Uh, sure."

"I brought Tyler here so she could live out her last few months in nature. She loved the woods. Then, one morning she just... disappeared. And then the animals changed. They started coming to the cabin when they were hurt, like they knew who I was, like they knew I could help them." Piper's eyes were beginning to water. "I started to think that maybe they were Tyler, somehow. In spirit, you know? I realize that's a ridiculous thing to think, but I've been living here permanently ever since, to take care of the animals. I couldn't leave them."

"I don't think that's ridiculous," said Cyrena, awkwardly putting her hand on Piper's back to comfort her.

"The lake changed soon after that, and it's been slowly getting worse. I don't like to think about it."

"You don't like to think about the lake?"

"The animals and the lake both changed around the same time Tyler disappeared. If Tyler's spirit is in the animals, is she also in the lake? I... don't know what to do with those thoughts."

Cyrena began rolling the bullet between her fingers again. "Piper, do the animals ever talk to you?"

"Uh, no?" Piper's face held a confused look, which then turned to annoyance. "What are you saying?"

"Oh, I'm sorry! I'm not making fun of you. The animals have been talking to me. I wasn't sure how to bring it up."

"The animals *talk to you?* What do they say?"

"A fox told me where you lived after I got shot, and a squirrel helped me find the bullet."

Piper stood up very suddenly, knocking her chili bowl to the ground. "Did they say anything else about me? Do you think they could be Tyler?"

"The fox said you're kind to animals, but that was it. It wasn't a long conversation. And when I asked the fox their name, they didn't say Tyler. They specifically didn't want to be called by a human name."

"Oh. Okay. Yes, alright. This is a lot to process." Piper picked up her dropped chili bowl and took it to the kitchen.

Cyrena finished the rest of her chili in silence, and then brought her bowl to Piper. "Thanks for the food. It was very garlic. Very, very garlic."

"Do you think the animals could be Tyler?"

"No. I don't know for sure, but I don't think so."

"What about…" Piper paused for a moment, and then looked Cyrena directly in the eyes. "What about the lake?"

"No. I don't think Tyler became an evil lake, either."

Piper washed the bowls, and stacked them on a shelf. When she turned around to face Cyrena again, her face was full of dread. "I'm worried," said Piper, "that maybe it was Tyler who shot you."

"Why would you think that?"

"The silver. She liked making stuff. She would make me pendants and charms out of smelted silver and gold. So, she could have made the bullet. And a few weeks after she disappeared, the rifle we kept in the cabin disappeared too." Piper's eyes were beginning to water again. "I don't know. None of this makes any sense. It's been years, there's no way she's even still alive."

"I mean, that's a hell of a coincidence, but can you think of any reason why she would want to shoot me? With silver bullets?"

"No. I can't."

There was a scratch at the cabin door, and both Cyrena and Piper jumped.

"That sounds like an animal," said Piper, who rushed to the door, "they show up at all hours."

Piper opened the door, and sitting silently on the porch was Nameless, looking statuesque and purposeful.

"It's a fox!" said Piper, waving Cyrena over.

Cyrena walked to the door and looked down at Nameless. "Oh, hello Nameless. Good to see you again."

Nameless looked up at Cyrena, and said, "We must

visit the owls. Just us. The doctor cannot understand our words."

Cyrena looked over at Piper, who had not reacted at all to what the fox said. "I need to go, Piper, but I'll be back."

"Oh. Okay. Of course," said Piper, sounding disappointed.

Nameless stood up and began to walk, slowly, into the woods.

"Can you ask the animals if they know anything about Tyler?" asked Piper, as Cyrena stepped outside.

"Sure, I'll find out what I can."

"Oh! And ask them if they knew my dog, Peaches. She was a good dog."

"I'm probably not going to ask them about your dog."

"Okay. Yeah. Priorities! Have a good time in the woods!"

Cyrena followed behind Nameless, and within moments they had disappeared into the dark of night.

CHAPTER FIVE

Wisdom of the Owls

The sky was thick with clouds, and without the light of the moon the woods had fallen into complete darkness. Cyrena stumbled around blindly, gently holding on to Nameless' tail as they journeyed deeper and deeper into the forest.

"I should have brought a flashlight," said Cyrena, tripping over a root.

"I'm sorry, I did not realize you would be unable to see," said Nameless.

The forest was as quiet as it had been during the day. There were no crickets, or rustling leaves, or any sounds at all besides the soft pattering of paws from Nameless, and the unsteady clomping of boots from Cyrena.

"Piper wanted me to ask you about her partner, Tyler," said Cyrena. "She's supposed to be dead, but, you know, so am I. Do you know her?"

Nameless slowed for a moment. "Yes. It was Tyler who shot you."

Cyrena let go of Nameless' tail. "Wait, what?"

Nameless continued walking, and Cyrena slowly stumbled forward, blindly. "I wasn't sure, when we first met. But I am certain now. Tyler tried to kill you, and I believe she will try again."

Cyrena tripped and fell to the ground. "Hold up, I need your tail."

"Of course."

Cyrena heard a delicate rustling in front of her, and then felt a soft, furry tail brush against her arm. "Thanks," she said, grabbing it.

"It was Tyler who led the animals of these woods to the kind doctor, and told us of her healing skills. Tyler looks after us, protects us—out of love for the doctor, I believe. I do not know where Tyler is now, but the owls will know. The owls see everything."

"I've always wanted to talk to an owl."

"I find them frustrating. Most birds are cordial, pleasant. But not owls. Owls are... difficult."

Cyrena noticed a faint, flickering glow up ahead. It was the first thing she had been able to see since leaving the cabin.

"There. Owls," said Nameless.

"Are those..."

"Candles."

The area ahead was dotted with candles. Big candles, small candles, some of them molded into interesting shapes, some of them dyed bright colors. At least two dozen trees were covered in them, and they were arranged in strange, sloppy patterns all across the forest floor. Thick, melted wax was dripping everywhere, and a uniquely unpleasant combination of scents wafted through the air.

"This seems dangerous," said Cyrena, looking around in awe at the dazzling and beautiful fire hazard.

"Very, whoo-whooooo! Very dangerous indeed, whooooo! Whoo whooo whoooooo," boomed an extremely owl-sounding voice from out of a nearby tree.

"Owls, this human has come seeking information," said Nameless, ears sticking up, eyes darting from tree to tree.

"Whooooo are you, human? I am an owl, whoooooo, but whooooo are you?"

Nameless, eyes scowling, looked at Cyrena. "This *who-ing* thing is new. I think it's for your benefit."

"Whooooo, no, this is regular owl talk, yes, whooooooo!" A large white barn owl flew down from one of the trees, and landed heavily on Cyrena's shoulder.

"Oh! Hello there," said Cyrena, bewildered.

"Yes, whooo! I am an owl! Look at me, whooooo!" The owl jumped off Cyrena's shoulder, flew around for a moment, and then landed on her other shoulder. "My name is Owl. I'm an owl, yes, whooo."

A brown horned owl flew down from another tree, and landed forcefully on Cyrena's head. "Whoooo-wait a minute! My name is Owl and I am also an owl, whoooo!"

"Okay," said Cyrena, agitated. "Nice to meet you both."

The barn owl looked up at the horned owl, and then at Cyrena. "Whoooo, do not believe the horned owl's lies! Their name is Raven! Raven, the owl!"

The horned owl jumped off Cyrena's head and flapped

their wings wildly at the barn owl. *"Your* name is Raven, whooooo! My name is *Owl,* the *Pure.* The *Grand.* Whoooo!"

Both owls took off into the air, zigzagging around the trees, trying to scratch each other.

Nameless looked up at Cyrena, and said, "Every owl is like this. Every single owl."

"I should hope so, whooo!" yelled the barn owl.

"Every owl is perfection, whooo!" screeched the horned owl.

"Every owl is divine and saintly, as if an angel upon the Earth, woooo!" screamed the barn owl.

"We are looking for Tyler, the sentinel of the lake," said Nameless, their voice loud and steady.

The owls swooped over to a tree, each grabbing a large candle with their powerful claws. Then, candles in grasp, they began to circle Cyrena, the whirling light creating a disorientating strobe effect around her.

"Yes, whoooo! Tyler the watcher, Tyler the protector, whooo!" menaced the barn owl.

"Tyler is coming for you, human! Whooo-man! Ha ha! Whoooo-man!" laughed the horned owl.

"Oh no!" yelled the barn owl, dropping their candle. "Whoooo-old on a second!" The barn owl flew into a tree and grabbed another candle, then flew back into formation with the horned owl. "I dropped my candle, but I have found another, whoooo!"

"They are not usually quite this spirited," said Nameless, grumpily.

The barn owl dropped their candle a second time, and as the lit wick hit the ground it ignited a small pile of leaves.

"Whooooo-nooooooo!" yelled both owls, simultaneously.

"What whoooo-ve I done?" yelled the barn owl, whose flying became erratic.

"You-whooo-ve doomed us all, whooooo!" yelled the horned owl.

A tiny fire formed around the candle. Cyrena ran over to the flame and stomped it out with her boots.

"Whoo-ray, you have saved the forest!" yelled the barn owl.

The horned owl flew over to Cyrena, holding a small twig, and placed the twig upon her head. "Queen of the Woods, we dub thee. Whoooo-p whoooo-p whoooo-ray!"

"From this day forward, humans shall be known as friends of the owls! Whoooooo, yes! Good friends, whoooo!" said the barn owl, hopping from tree to tree.

"Please, owl friends, where can I find Tyler?" asked Cyrena, flustered.

"Under the earth, whoooo!" said the barn owl.

"Under a door of wood! Whoo-whoo-whoo!" sang the horned owl.

Nameless looked to Cyrena. "There is a bunker north of the lake, near where a cabin once stood. I believe that is what the owls are referring to."

The two owls fell to the ground, and began rolling around in the dirt and melted wax.

"She slumbers by day, and haunts the woods by night, whoo-whoo!" screeched the barn owl, rolling up to Cyrena's feet.

"Mornings are best, for your quest! Seek her then, or

be shot again! I'm rhyming now, whooo!" said the horned owl, with a laugh.

"Thank you for your assistance," said Nameless, turning around. "Come Cyrena, I will return you to the cabin."

"Thank you owls. And be careful with the candles!" Cyrena waved to the owls and began to walk away.

"We will not squander this gift you have given us, this precious gift of life, whoooo!" yelled the horned owl, still rolling around in the dirt.

"We will live a life of chaste service to the gods of nature, whooo! We repent! We repent!" shouted the barn owl, flying up into one of the trees.

Both owls then yelled, in a frenzied, imperfect unison, "Never forget us, and we shall live on forever in your heart, whoooooo!"

CHAPTER SIX

The Death of Cyrena Shade

There was a small break in the clouds, and the woods were now faintly illuminated by a cold, blue moonlight. Nameless' gray fur had an almost phosphorescent glow in this light, and Cyrena followed the glow as she carefully stepped around shrubs and trees.

"I appreciate all you're doing for me, Nameless," said Cyrena, ducking under a low-hanging branch.

"It is not a selfless act. I seek knowledge, and you possess knowledge that I do not."

"I think I'm beginning to piece together why I was shot. And if I'm right, I might know what's wrong with the lake."

Nameless turned their head slightly. "Are you willing to share your thoughts?"

"Not yet, not about the lake, not until I'm certain. But I can tell you why I can't die. You've definitely earned that much, Nameless." Cyrena stepped into a wet, slimy puddle, and her foot sunk down into the mud.

"I am eager to listen, human."

Cyrena pulled up her leg, shook the muck from her boot, and then took a deep, melancholy breath. "I did die, once. Genuinely, completely died, about thirty years ago. It was such a quick, trivial thing."

*   *   *

There was a cool autumn rain lightly sprinkling the amber treetops. It was just enough rain to make everything damp, but not enough to discourage Cyrena from taking her usual walk. She wasn't walking anywhere in particular, she just enjoyed being outside in places where she was unlikely to run into other people. It was a gray, dreary day, but the trees were beautiful this time of year, and it was not yet unbearably cold.

As Cyrena walked along the remains of a forgotten, overgrown path, she heard the unmistakable meow of a distressed cat. Without thinking, she decided to meow back. "Meow?"

She heard it a second time—a pained meow, from an unseen area to the right. She walked toward the sound of the cat, through thick, damp foliage, trying not to rip her gray jacket on the branches.

"Meow?" she said, and again the cat meowed in response.

It was coming from up in the trees. Cyrena's eyes darted from tree to tree, until she spotted a thin, orange tabby huddled on a branch far above. The cat was dirty and matted, and had what looked like a small gash on their face directly above their right eye. They were wearing a collar, Cyrena noticed, which meant that the cat was likely lost, and not accustomed to life in the woods.

"Hello, kitty!" said Cyrena, in a calm, friendly voice. "Are you stuck up there, cat friend?"

The cat meowed twice, and then shifted slightly.

"It's okay, kitty. I'll help you down, and get you home. Is that okay?"

The cat meowed again, and looked down hopefully at Cyrena.

It was a very large tree the cat had climbed, but it looked sturdy, and had lots of twisty branches. A good climbing tree, thought Cyrena. She took off her jacket and began slowly scaling its trunk.

"I'm coming, kitty," said Cyrena, grabbing onto the first branch and pulling herself up. The cat watched intently, no longer meowing. In less than a minute Cyrena had just about reached the cat, who was looking hopeful and desperate. "Almost there, kitty," said Cyrena, as she tried to figure out her next move.

What occurred next happened very quickly. Cyrena was turning herself around when the branch she was standing on made a snapping sound and jerked downward. It had shifted only slightly, but it was enough to make Cyrena lose her footing. She tumbled off the branch and landed on the ground in an extraordinarily unlucky position, breaking her neck and killing her almost instantly.

Everything went black for Cyrena. And then, just as swiftly, everything came back into focus. She was standing next to the tree, breathing, moving, thinking.

"What... happened?" she said to herself, looking around anxiously.

As she looked to the spot where she had fallen, her question was answered. Lying in the wet leaves was her own body, limbs sprawled, neck misshapen.

"Oh, jeez," she said, stumbling back. "Oh no. That's... I died. Alright. Wow."

A strange feeling began to burrow into Cyrena. It felt like every inch of her was being watched, like there was a warm gaze on her skin. It was an uncomfortable, invasive feeling.

The tabby in the tree started hissing aggressively, and in the distance Cyrena could see an advancing figure. At first it was just a dark, fuzzy blur, but as it drew closer the figure became unnervingly clear. He was a huge, lumbering wolf with patchy black and white fur, walking slowly on two hulking hind legs. He wore a peculiar black cloak, made of the darkest material Cyrena had ever seen. In the wolf's right paw was a twisty, thick piece of wood, burnt on one end, but smooth and almost glass-like on the other. It looked to Cyrena like a sort of wand.

As the wolf arrived in front of her, Cyrena found herself unable to run, or speak, or do anything. The beast was very tall, towering at least three feet above her head. He was also very old, and Cyrena watched in alarm as patches of hair slowly fell off his face and arms.

The wolf raised his wand, and the burnt end ignited in an unnatural purple flame. As this happened, a large ovular shape, purple and bright, ripped into the air next to them.

Cyrena stared apprehensively at the strange ethereal

portal, and then looked back at the wolf. "Do you want me to go in there?" she asked.

The wolf nodded his head, eyes unblinking, gaze fixed on Cyrena.

"Okay, sure." Cyrena slowly approached the glowing oval. There was a cold, lifeless feeling about it that worried her. The wolf stepped forward, and Cyrena hastily jumped through, not wanting to be forced in.

Everything inside the oval was a misty, dark gray, giving Cyrena the harrowing impression that she was no longer anywhere. At first she thought the grayness felt cold, but after a moment she realized that was she was actually feeling was nothing—it was no temperature at all.

The wolf entered into the gray realm behind her, and then slowly journeyed ahead, beckoning her to follow. As Cyrena followed the old beast through the mist, and away from the ovular purple doorway, she began to fully comprehend the truth of what was happening. She had died, and was being ferried into the afterlife.

Tears began welling up in Cyrena's eyes. What would her mother do when she found out? Would her father even care? Cyrena hadn't seen him since she was a toddler.

The wolf let out a thick, gravely cough, and more of his fur fell off, disappearing into the misty gray. Though he was enormous and had a menacing scowl, Cyrena thought he looked rather frail and tired.

They walked and walked, although the scenery did not change. They were still in a thick gray mist, and there was nothing but gray mist ahead of them. Cyrena's eyes dried up, and she began to feel a deep, hollow numbness.

The wolf coughed again, this time much more violently,

and the force of the cough caused him to drop his wand. Fatigued, he looked to the ground, searching the mist with his old, glassy eyes.

"Do you need help finding it?" asked Cyrena, but the wolf did not respond.

Cyrena stood silently as the wolf got onto his knees and began patting the misty floor, looking for his missing wand. Another fit of coughing began, which turned into a sickly wheeze, and then the wolf fell over onto his side.

Cyrena bent down next to the wolf, not sure what she should do. "Are you okay? How can I help?"

The wolf was breathing in gasps, and the remainder of his fur fell from his withering face. His eyes looked drained and worried.

Cyrena searched around for the wand, and found it near the wolf's legs. It was warm, and much heavier than she had expected. She lifted the wand and rested it in the wolf's giant right paw. Then, using both of her hands, she closed his paw tightly around it.

"There, your wand, I found it," she said.

The wolf's breathing slowed, and he looked at her with a strange, almost apologetic stare. Soon his breathing stopped entirely, and his eyes glossed into a blank, mindless gaze. The wolf was dead.

Cyrena collapsed on the ground next to him, stunned. What was she supposed to do now? Where had the wolf been taking her? Could she get there by herself? Should she wait for another wolf?

She waited next to the dead wolf for hours, but no one came. She yelled for help, but no one heard. She was alone, in an infinite gray mist, and no one was coming to save her.

"Alright. Alright. You have to do something," Cyrena said to herself. "The wolf was leading you somewhere. There has to be a way out."

She looked at the strange wand in the wolf's paw. There was still a faint, ember-like glow on the burnt end. The wolf had used it to open a doorway, so maybe she could do the same. With an immense yank she pulled it from the wolf's tight grasp, and examined it in her hands. How did it work? Did it channel a power that the wolf had, or did it contain a power of its own?

Cyrena waved the wand around, focusing her mind on thoughts of opening an ethereal doorway, but nothing happened. Over and over again she tried to make the wand do something, anything, but if it contained any power it was not yielding it to her.

Exasperated, she sat down and rested against the colossal, dead beast. His cloak, she noticed, was also magical looking. It was unnaturally black—so black that she could not discern anything about its material besides the color. Was the cloak required for the wand to work?

It took hours to get the cloak completely off of the enormous, death-stiff wolf. It was soft and delicate feeling, and it ripped and teared as she removed it. "Oh god, I hope I'm not ruining it," muttered Cyrena. But by the time the task was complete, the cloak had mysteriously repaired itself.

The incredible garment was many sizes too big for her, but as she pulled it over her head it seemed to shrink, and soon the cloak had reformed itself into a properly fitted dress. "Progress," said Cyrena, relieved that something positive had happened.

She tried using the wand again, but nothing came of it. Maybe she needed to be in the right place for it to work? Where could the right place possibly be? She looked around desperately, but there was nothing to be seen but gray.

Cyrena set off into the mist, not sure where she was going but determined to go somewhere. As she walked she waved the wand around, hoping to accidentally stumble upon a spot where it might actually do something. An hour went by, and then another. How big could this place be? "It's not infinite," she said to herself, "because that would be a nightmare."

There was something in the distance, a sparkle, a tiny speck of light. Or was it just her desperate imagination? She ran toward it. It was real, and getting brighter as she approached. A light, a glow, a purple glow! An ethereal doorway, like the one she had walked through to get here! Or, perhaps it *was* the doorway she had walked through to get here—the doorway that led back to the tree, to her dead body.

"Well, hopefully this doesn't lead somewhere even worse. Good luck, me," said Cyrena. She patted herself on the shoulder, took a deep, apprehensive breath, and jumped through the purple light.

* * *

Cyrena and Nameless were nearly back to the cabin—the warm light from the cabin's windows pierced invitingly through the trees ahead.

"After I jumped through," said Cyrena, "I woke up in my mangled body. The doorway was gone, and the black dress and wand were lying on the ground near the tree. After a few absolutely *agonizing* hours my neck managed to fix itself, and I walked home. I've died three times since then. Twice, unbelievably, via lake murder. But when I die now I just come right back."

"What happened to the cat?" asked Nameless.

"Oh, yeah! The cat had gotten down on their own, the jerk! I grabbed them and was able to find their owners, so they got home alright too."

"Do you still have the wand?"

"Nah. For the longest time I tried to figure out how to work it, but it never did anything magical for me. And then I lost it in a fire. The wand couldn't repair itself like the dress."

They arrived at the cabin just as the moon fell behind another cloud. Nameless sat on the porch and looked up at Cyrena. "Thank you for telling me your story, human. May I ask one more question of you?"

"Sure," said Cyrena.

"Why did you come to Blackmore Lake?"

Cyrena sighed. "I don't age, and I'm worried that I'll never die. I don't *want* to die, but I'm way more terrified of not being *able* to die. So, I've been traveling around, looking for death. Looking for another wolf."

Cyrena stared into the darkness, her gaze pointed in the direction of the distant lake.

"Something has been pulling me here, to these woods, to that lake. Standing near the lake... I can feel the same penetrating warmness on my skin that I felt when the wolf first arrived to take me away. Death, it's here. It's in Blackmore Lake."

CHAPTER SEVEN

Sisters in Death

As soon as the sun began to rise, Cyrena and Piper set off northward into the woods. The sky was still cloudy and gray, and a faint drizzle was keeping the ground unpleasantly muddy. Birds were screeching aggressively in the distance, and every few minutes there was a low, rumbling thunder.

Cyrena had explained what she learned to Piper, who found the information confusing and painful. Why had Tyler let Piper think that she was dead? Why was she shooting people with silver bullets at the lake? Cyrena had a theory, but she kept it to herself. There were many things that still didn't make sense.

"The bunker should be over this hill," said Piper. "The cabin is mostly gone now. It was already abandoned when I started coming here as a kid. I stepped on a nail once, goofing off inside it. My mother didn't let me play there anymore after that."

As they reached the top of the hill, the remnants of a

small log cabin came into view. Only half a wall remained—the rest was now a crumbled pile of rotted wood.

"That's it. The bunker is somewhere behind it. It was a tornado shelter, I think."

They walked down the hill toward the cabin, and then circled around the old, decaying logs. A wooden hatch in the ground came into view—it looked heavy and old, and had a rusted metal handle and a busted latch.

Piper was breathing heavily, her eyes fixed on the hatch. She seemed to be on the verge of passing out. "Open it," she said. "I need to see. Open it."

Cyrena grabbed the rusty, wet handle, and with one huge heave she swung the door open.

Piper exhaled sharply, and began to tear up. "She's not here. God, she's not here. That's definitely our gun, though," said Piper, pointing at a rifle on the floor of the bunker.

Someone *was* there, though. Sitting against the wall of the bunker was a frail looking woman, wearing a dirty button-down shirt and dark gray jeans. She had short brown hair and tired green eyes, which were staring fiercely at Cyrena.

"She can't see me," said the woman. "What I want to know is why she *can* see *you.*"

Cyrena looked at Piper, who was wiping tears off onto her sleeve.

"What now?" asked Piper. "Do we wait here? Do we come back?"

"We should probably talk privately, Cyrena," said the woman in the bunker.

"Go back to the cabin," said Cyrena to Piper. "I'll be back soon."

Once Piper had disappeared over the hill, Cyrena stepped down into the bunker.

"I'm Tyler," said the woman, still sitting against the wall.

"Yeah, I guessed."

"Sorry for shooting you. I thought you were one of *them*. I saw you wearing that black... *thing*, and thought maybe they could look like people."

"You've seen a cloaked wolf, then?" asked Cyrena.

"Yeah, after I died in the lake. Are you like me, then? A ghost? Why can Piper see you?"

"I'm not sure. When I died, a giant cloaked wolf came to collect me, and he brought me to this weird, barren, misty gray nothingness. But soon after we got there, the wolf just... *died*."

Tyler's eyes widened. "That's what happened to me! The wolf brought me to that... place, and then it fell over dead, and I came back here through the hole. But you're like... a whole person. I'm a ghost. I can sort of... move stuff around, but no one except the animals can see or hear me."

Cyrena thought very carefully. What was different about their deaths? About what happened to them *after* their deaths?

"How did you die, exactly?" asked Cyrena.

"Oh, boy. Piper had this dog, Peaches, and she was super old. I would take her swimming out at the lake in the morning. Well, one day we were swimming and she starts convulsing, like she's having a seizure or something. I swim over and try to grab her, to bring her to shore, and all of a sudden she stops convulsing and starts getting all aggressive. Biting and scratching and stuff. I let go, but by that point

I had swallowed a bunch of water, and was choking. Next thing I know I'm sinking, feeling light headed. And I start to think… maybe I shouldn't try to swim back up."

Tyler shifted uncomfortably.

"I had cancer, right? The treatment for it hadn't worked, and I had like… six months left, max. It was going to suck for Piper, taking care of me through that. So I thought, maybe this is better. Just let it end here. So I didn't fight it, and I drowned. And then some monster wolf dude dragging me into a hole in the lake."

A thought was beginning to form in Cyrena's head. "Tyler, what did you do with the wolf's wand and cloak?"

"What? I didn't touch any of that stuff. I just ran back out of the hole when the wolf croaked."

Cyrena began pacing excitedly. "When you left the gray place, did you find yourself back in your body?"

"No, my corpse was still lying there on the lakebed. That night I dragged it out so Piper wouldn't find it. I buried myself right behind this bunker. What a weird night *that* was."

Cyrena knelt down in front of Tyler, eyes blazing. "And what about the hole? Is it still there?"

"As far as I know. At least it was the last time I checked."

"Tyler. Tyler I'm so sorry. But you're in for a terrible time."

"What? Why?"

"Because we're going to close up the hole, and when we do your body is going to slowly and painfully recompose."

Tyler studied Cyrena's face, as if trying to determine if she was serious or not. "Oh. Damn. Alright. We should probably dig me up first, then."

CHAPTER EIGHT

Into the Lake

Blackmore Lake was looking especially grim. A thin film of sludge lined the top of the water like an infected skin, and a sickly black foam had collected along the lake's edges. It was possibly the most unpleasant body of water in the entire world.

Cyrena and Tyler approached the lake with a hurried determination. "Do you remember where the doorway is?" asked Cyrena.

Tyler pointed at the center of the water. "It's around the middle there. But it's flat against the lakebed, so we might need to dig for it if too much sludge has built up."

The smell of the lake was overwhelming, and Cyrena was not looking forward to swimming in it again, but she could see no other option. "Alright, well, let's start looking."

She took a quick, deep breath, closed her eyes, and jumped into the thick, slimy abyss. Tyler followed soon after, her spectral body barely affecting the water as she waded through it.

Cyrena reached the middle of the lake, near the spot where she had recently died, and began digging through the sticky silt. The warmness on her skin was intensifying, and she knew the doorway must be nearby. Tyler was swimming around effortlessly, occasionally sticking her hands down into the muck, but finding nothing.

After about a minute, Cyrena stopped digging and swam to the surface for oxygen. The air around the lake was thick and foul, and Cyrena was surprised by how painful it was to breathe. "Gaaahhh, gross," she muttered, and then sank back down into the poison pool to continue her search.

Cyrena's eyes were starting to hurt, and she wasn't sure how much more of the lake she could handle. As she plunged her hand into the oozy silt again, she felt something peculiar that she couldn't quite interpret. She dug her other hand into the filth, and could feel more of the same strange shape. This wasn't the ethereal door, it was something physical, intricate, firm. She grabbed onto the mysterious object with both hands and pulled on it with all of her strength. Out of the silt popped dozens of tangled animal skeletons—birds, and rabbits, and squirrels. Distressingly, each skeleton had a mutilated, ripped, torn up skull.

Cyrena gasped and began to choke on the toxic lake water. Tyler, realizing what was happening, bolted to her side and rushed her to the surface. Cyrena spat up some water and then breathed heavily, trying to regain her composure. She looked around angrily into the trees surrounding the lake.

"Squirrel!" Cyrena yelled. "You're a monster, squirrel!"

The hollow voice of the face-eating squirrel echoed across the lake from a location unknown. "Now you know my true terrible secret! It's that my terrible secret was true!"

"I swear to god, if I see you again I'll stomp you to death with my bare feet!"

"I need to be true to myself! I'm a face eater! I love eating face meat, day and night! I'm going to keep eating faces as long as I live! You had your chance to stop me, but now you never will!"

Cyrena yelled murderously at the squirrel, and desperately wanted to search the woods and strangle them, but she had more important things to focus on.

"Sorry," said Cyrena to Tyler. "We should keep searching."

"Oh, I found it!" said Tyler. "Right before you started yelling at that squirrel."

"What? Amazing! Let's go then."

They sank once more into the murky waters, and Cyrena saw it immediately—a small, glowing, purple light peaking from beneath the silt. They dug through the impossibly thick sludge and uncovered the rest of the ghostly doorway, its other-worldly light shining bright through the rotten water. Tyler looked to Cyrena, and they both gave each other a thumbs up. Then, without another thought, they plunged themselves through the ethereal passageway.

Cyrena had forgotten how intensely nothing-like the

gray mist felt. It emptied you, it hollowed you out. It was as if you were being diluted, or slowly washed away.

"This place sucks," said Tyler, and she waved a middle finger at the mist.

"Yeah, no wonder the lake got all messed up, with this nonsense leaking out into it."

"Look, over there," said Tyler, pointing to a black dot in the distance. "That's the wolf."

Tyler's wolf hadn't made it nearly as far as Cyrena's before dying, so it didn't take long for them to reach the animal's body, which was now an oozing, decomposing mess.

"Gross," said Tyler.

"Weird. There's… no skeleton," noticed Cyrena.

It was true—there were no bones to be found in the strange, gooey remains of the wolf creature.

"I've got the wand," said Tyler, lifting a long wooden wand out of the sticky pile that was once the wolf's paw.

"I think, given the state of the body, it'll be easier if we rip the cloak off. It should repair itself," said Cyrena.

"Do we *need* to take the cloak?"

"I don't know. But I don't think we should risk leaving it. Also, I think you should wear it out of here, because that's what I did."

"Wonderful."

Cyrena and Tyler each grabbed one side of the cloak, and began tearing it from the wolf's blob-like remains. The smell, somehow, was even worse than the smell of the lake.

After a few good minutes of tearing and pulling, the cloak was free, and they laid the sticky fabric on the ground in a heap.

"Just leave it there for a minute before putting it on, it should clean itself," said Cyrena.

Sure enough, a few minutes later the cloak had cleaned itself up, and stitched itself back together. Tyler pulled the strange garment over her head, and it began to shrink itself around her body, forming into an intensely black pair of coveralls.

"Oh, thank god it's not a dress," said Tyler.

Cyrena looked around the grayness, trying to notice something she hadn't the first time she was here, but there was nothing. It was a misty void. There were no clues to be found.

"You okay?" asked Tyler.

"Yeah. I just wish there were answers for me here. Oh well. When you're ready, we'll head back through the hole. If I'm right about this, the doorway will shut, and you'll wake up back in your body as it slowly rebuilds itself."

"How much does it hurt?"

"It's the worst. Pain on an unimaginable scale. You will never forget the feeling, you'll carry it with you forever."

"Alright. Got it." Tyler screamed aggressively and ran toward the ethereal doorway, waving two middle fingers wildly in the air.

CHAPTER NINE

Onward, Forever

It took three full days for Tyler's body to reform. Piper stayed by her side for every terrible moment, and did what she could to lessen the pain, but it was still agony, and there were moments when Tyler wished she had remained a ghost.

The lake had begun clearing up almost immediately after the doorway was closed, and within a few weeks the dark sludge had all but disappeared. The animals, Cyrena was disappointed to find, no longer seemed to possess the ability to speak. Or, possibly, she herself could simply no longer hear them.

Piper's disposition had changed dramatically—having Tyler back was like having a piece of her soul returned. Cyrena was glad to see her so unequivocally joyful, but being close to that joy was difficult, as Cyrena knew that such happiness was not something she herself would likely ever experience.

Piper and Tyler offered to let Cyrena stay at the cabin with them as long as she wanted, but Cyrena knew that she had to leave. Her search was not nearly complete.

"I'll be heading out tomorrow," said Cyrena over dinner one night. "That feeling that led me here, to the doorway in the lake, I can feel it again. I think that means there's another door open, somewhere."

"How many people do you think get taken away by wolves when they die?" asked Tyler. "And how many of those wolves just straight up die themselves? *On the job?*"

"If I ever find answers to those questions I'll let you know," said Cyrena.

"Oh," said Piper, "apparently you have Tyler to thank for tonight's meal. And all of the meals."

"What? Why's that?" asked Cyrena.

Tyler laughed. "Piper thought that occasionally remembering to water the vegetables was resulting in a perfectly maintained and fertilized garden."

"Everything was growing fine, so I thought I was doing all the farming stuff right! I didn't realize there was a friendly ghost tending to it every day."

Cyrena laughed. And then she felt a small, somber sting, realizing that she hadn't had a pleasant laugh in a long, long time.

* * *

The walk from the cabin back to the highway was quite lengthy, so the next morning Cyrena left as early as she could. It was a gorgeous day—the sky was clear, and the sun cascaded pleasantly across the swaying treetops, creating a sparkling display of light and color.

Cyrena trekked up a small hill toward a path in the distance, thinking about the strange, penetrating warmth on her skin that would point her in the direction of the next doorway. Helping Tyler had given her some interesting new theories, but she still didn't have the answers she so desperately desired.

"Oh!" said Cyrena in surprise, as she realized that Nameless was sitting next to a tree in front of her. "I'm sorry, I was deep inside my own head, I didn't notice you were there. Hello!"

Nameless didn't respond.

"I guess we can't talk anymore. Well, in case you can still understand me, thank you for all your help, Nameless. I would pet you, but I have no idea if you like that sort of thing. Also you might just be a wild fox now."

Nameless watched her for a moment, and then looked up into the branches of an old, towering tree.

"Is there something in the tree? Did you want me to climb it? I don't really climb trees anymore, unless I really have to."

There was a rustling of leaves from a high, hidden branch. Cyrena squinted, but couldn't see what was making the sound. Suddenly a large, magnificent horned owl came bursting through the leaves. The owl swooped down in front of Cyrena and dropped something from their mighty claws, which landed on the ground with a squishy thud and then rolled up against her left boot. It was the bloody, severed head of the face-eating squirrel.

Made in the USA
Monee, IL
23 October 2020

45870244R00032